The Night Before the New Baby

Grosset & Dunlap

For my little babies—Sabaka, Toonces, Jemima and King Midas —N. W.

For my new niece or nephew, who was already supposed to be here—we're all waiting! Also, for Mel and Devin, who were the inspiration for this book. CONGRATULATIONS! —T. L.

Text copyright © 2002 by Natasha Wing. Illustrations copyright © 2002 by Tammie Lyon. All rights reserved. Published by Grosset & Dunlap, a division of Penguin Putnam Books for Young Readers, 345 Hudson Street, New York, NY 10014. GROSSET & DUNLAP is a trademark of Penguin Putnam Inc. Published simultaneously in Canada. Printed in the U.S.A.

Library of Congress Cataloging-in-Publication Data is available.

ISBN 0-448-42656-0   A B C D E F G H I J

The Night Before the New Baby

By Natasha Wing
Illustrated by Tammie Lyon

Grosset & Dunlap, Publishers

'Twas the night before the baby
decided to come,
Mom's belly was big and
as tight as a drum.

We'd painted and papered
the nursery with care,
in hopes that the new baby
soon would be there.

We bought a new dresser
some diapers, a bib.
We moved in the rocker
and set up the crib.

I picked out a mobile
and a special stuffed toy
to give to my sister
(but it could be a boy).

Mom's suitcase was ready
for the hospital rush,
packed with some nightgowns,
toothpaste and toothbrush.

All night my poor mother
felt pangs in her belly,
"Dad's calling the doctor.
I have to go, Nelly."

Grandma came over,
then Dad started the car.

He said, "Thank goodness
the doctor's not far."

Mom said in a panic,
"I'd better hurry!"
With a kiss and a hug
they left in a flurry.

I played cards with Grandma
and watched movies, too.
We made a big banner
that said, "We Love You."

My grandma then tucked me
all snug in my bed,
while visions of baby names
danced in my head.

I woke when the phone rang
and heard such a clatter,
I sprang from my bed
and asked, "What's the matter?"

Grandma was jumping,
her face beaming with joy,
"Tell me! Tell me!
Is it a girl or a boy?"

Off to the hospital—
it was just a short drive.
The nurse quickly brought us
to Room 285.

When what to our
wondering eyes should appear,
but a beautiful baby
who was finally here.

Those eyes—how they twinkled!
Those fat cheeks, how shiny!
The hair was like satin.
The nose was so tiny!

The pink pouty mouth
was the shape of an "o."
And I marveled at the size
of that weensy big toe.

Mom said, "Come say hello
to your new little sister."
I gave her the bunny,
then I hugged and I kissed her.

Dad asked, "Did you pick out
any good names?"
Grandma laughed and said,
"Forget Robert and James!"

I said, "I like Ann,
Sophie, and Josie.
But since she's so sweet.
Let's call her Rosie!"